FUN CAMP

PUBLISHING GENIUS PRESS
Baltimore, Maryland
www.publishinggenius.com

ISBN 13: 978-0-9887503-5-7

First printing: 2013
Book design by Adam Robinson
Forest collage by Stephanie Barber
Editorial consideration by J.A. Tyler

see also: www.gatherroundchildren.com

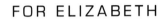
FOR ELIZABETH

MONDAY

NO MOMS FOR MILES

Best to think of the "rules" as opportunities. No coffee. No energy drinks. No unprescribed speed. No sharing prescribed speed. No unprescribed cola. No bowls, bongs, spliffs, one-hitters, some-hitters, kooks, ludes, spanks, syringes, or nards. No paraphernalia except in skits. No peanut butter within thirty feet of the following campers: Piper, Caden, Braden, Persephone, Big John, Little Jack, Tall Eddie, and all three Britneys. No flasks. No flask pockets. No trench coats. No unregistered firearms. No colors that have been gang colors. No gangs. No unprovoked limping. No weakness. No allergies. No glasses. No thinking of pulling the Prank of the Century and then not doing it. No heat strokes during afternoon rec hour. No exemptions from afternoon rec hour. No boys in girls' cabins. Leave room for the Spirit on the slow dance. Dance with everybody, especially the kitchen staff, especially poor, poor Puddy. In the event of confusing arousal, play some basketball. If that doesn't help, Nurse Nadine's muscle relaxants taste like Jolly Ranchers. If someone mocks you, laugh with them. During small groups, open up. During one-on-ones, be real. During quiet times, emote. No not singing. No unfun thoughts. No holding back. Half a forest got burned down for you to live it up.

SUMMER AFTER SUMMER OF LOVE

I'm even a little surprised at how good it is to see you.
It's silly how we didn't keep in touch all year like we
said we would. And a lot of the blame falls in my court,
considering you sent me that sweet letter in August
and then those less sweet letters September through
November. Notes I deserved, sure, but the issue being
that while I was still obsessing over my reply to that
first letter, trying to put to words exactly what I wanted
to say, I got that second letter, which *really* froze me
up. I had to shred the obsolete one and start all over.
It might've been wise to exchange phone numbers and
emails, but we'd bonded so much over Luddite anti-
tech stuff, it felt so romantic to just . . . And when your
third note arrived right as I was finishing *my* second,
which was getting really long and indulgent anyway,
I had to just throw the whole thing out. After that, the
school year got a hold of me, the upright bass, soccer
season, and I looked up and it was June. But on the van
ride over here, I started wondering if I'd see you, and
I had all these positive thoughts about you and about
the talks we had and about that last night of camp we
shared and the rashes we were so sure we'd get since
we couldn't see a damn thing so deep in the woods, and

about those sweet young promises we made to each other. Now here we are, smiling, all that stuff behind us, slates clean, fresh air, ready to laugh over new jokes. You've got to tell me what's been going on with you, but hey, first, I want you to meet my girlfriend.

THANK YOU BROTHER DAVE FOR THE KIND INTRODUCTION

Now heed. There was once a young man whose convictions led him to vegetarianism. At every feast he attended, even in the presence of potent men, he eschewed meat. What I'm getting at is: Are you daring to boldly go? Are you being spoon-fed, physically, in the spiritual sense? If you don't have anything you would die for, where then emotionally do you make your bed? Was it not the One Who Was who said, "You give them something to eat"? That abstinent young man's name, by the way, was Hitler, but maybe we all could take a page—and hit the Devil with it. What's your kampf? I mean that as a metaphor for struggle. You're all at stake here, and I don't mean Sizzler, Billy—I see Billy getting hungry over here; don't worry Billy not much longer. If you taste the voice of the Lord on your heart in this day or could just use someone to smack your lips at, won't you come forward as we stand. And as we sing.

YOU GOT TO GIVE TO GET

Across the deck outside the mess hall is a clothesline for pinning warm fuzzies, little notes to make co-campers' chests flutter with camaraderie. For example, a camper might write to me, "Dear Dave, Fun Camp is so great. I'm having the best time. Thank you for putting in so much work to make this a rewarding experience." To which I'd reply, "Dear Madeline, Quit sucking up to the staff and write a note to someone your own age. I don't need your validation, and neither does Fun Camp. It was here before you were born and will remain long after we're both dead." And now, look, we know each other better! All necessary paper, markers, glitter, and the whole bit await your creative destruction in the craft hut. Don't be that mopey kid going, "*Still* no warm fuzzies," and then when I ask how many you've given, you say, "Well…" Likewise, standing by the clothesline shouting "refresh inbox!" wastes lungs and connotes desperation. Remember, you campers with less personality, it really is a numbers game—if you write enough notes, you're gonna get a reply. Even telemarketers make a sale now and then.

ICE-BREAKER

You're riding an elevator with a vacantly beautiful woman who pulls a wad of cash from her purse and says to you, "I'm going to use this to purchase a goat, which I will sacrifice to Satan." Then she gets off the elevator and leaves the purse behind. Do you call out to her and return the purse? Do you remove the "goat money" and then return the purse? Do you keep the purse *and* the money, then run up her credit cards to be sure and disable her powers as a conduit of darkness? If so, would you only spend the money on donations to worthy charities or might you take a small portion of the money and buy a sandwich? And if that sandwich is a goat sandwich, are you really any better than the Satanist?

THE UNFUN AMONG US

I know you all like hanging with the cool kids, and why not? Cool is cool. But the cool are autonomous. All they need is a pat on the back and a "keep doing what you're doing." Make no mistake, counselors—the losers are our projects here, and we don't have much time. What makes this mentorship such a good deed is that the losers aren't going to like getting molded any more than you're gonna like molding. Unfun campers will absent themselves from contact with the staff any way they can think to: daydreams, fantasies, self-seclusion, negativism, loner-loitering, convulsive seizures, chronic sleepiness, and non-participation in activities such as skits, archery, rec hour, and Pranks of the Century. In our experience, persistent avoidance sends the message, "By absenting myself from fun, I will provoke you to retaliate. Your stern retribution will prove that you counselors are not as fun as you profess to be. Hence, you cannot help me." Bullhonkey. What the child really fears are his own boring impulses. And they will be broken.

Dear Mom,

I miss you. And Dad. And our house. And Johannes. Please show him pictures of me while feeding him treats. Please keep Deirdre out of my room and punish her if you catch her in there. I'm having some fun already but I don't know how I'll make it a whole week. A girl stole my hat but I got it back.

Love,

Billy

LET'S HEAR IT FOR THE PERMA-STAFF

These guys were here for the Jews the week before us, they're here for Fun Camp, and they'll be here next week, when we've all gone home to caption camp scrapbooks and the Junior Achievers show up to swap business cards, practice faking shame over international foibles, and generally treat this ranch like a convention center. So, briefly: Nurse Nadine here'll fix you up like a pro while honoring her belief in the Healing Power of Improvisational Storytelling. No examples just now please, Nadine. Save it for the wounded with no place to go. Chefs Grogg, Puddy, and Marimba will be dishing up all your high-protein fun fuel this week. Be sure and thank them—food staff have powers you just hope to God you're nice enough to keep them from using. That said, Grogg's a talker, so engage at your own risk. Same goes for Ole Sammy here, on paper a groundskeeper but in practice a cool drink-sipper who perches in the shade dispensing salty wisdom. This guy's sage as hell and has maybe even been in some wars? Sam? Sam's shaking his head. But just know, the perma-staff's got their own thing going. They won't be on-message like myself, Dave, Bernadette, and your counselors, so when they speak, be respectful and polite but be prepared to dismiss whatever they advocate as apocryphal. Likewise, they've asked that we not try to convert them this year, even while smiling, even when they could sorely use our message. We'll soon find out if they mean it.

THERE ARE LIMITS

Were you there when he got out of the lake, shimmering, holding a mackerel he caught by hand? Out of that dumpy muck somehow smelling better than ever, like melted butter with lemon? I *am* planning on waiting. He's only looked at me four times in two years. I'm simply saying that if Tad Gunnick took me on a nature stroll and pointed out various floras and faunas and told me that, frankly, clothes have always been a pet peeve of his, I'd do what I could not to bother him. And if that felt as good as he promised, and he laid out a soft velvet blanket like a gentleman and served me up a wine cooler, we would take it from there. There are limits to what a deft urbanite woman can barricade in the name of godly repute, is my point. Boy here likes you, he throws you in a pool. Boy here really likes you, God hums your name in his ear just as his dreams start to boil, then he approaches you somber at Quiet Time with big news he implies you can't decline. Back when I was in Girls Cabin 3, I got off on that just fine. But God must love a beauty in a spaghetti-string tank top cause my dream card filled up quick.

FREE TIME

You can get less than eight hours of sleep or more than eight hours of sleep or eight hours of sleep.

You can die alone or die addicted or go out to the bar tonight.

You can get diabetes or let fame make you boring or shoot hoops shirtless.

You can smile more or smile less or appear to be self-monitoring enough already.

You can tap on a wall or buy something that beeps or store your paintings on the hallway floor.

You can look up words you don't know or use context clues or you can read a book tonight.

You can say a prayer or sing a prayer or eat while it's hot.

You can pay one dollar for one donut or four dollars for six donuts or you can approach the dinner table with a clean conscience.

Monday

You can eat wax or be a hero or eat glue.

You can use me or define me or ask for my place of origin.

You can arrive early or arrive rested or you can think of yourself more as a searcher.

You can't or you won't, or in a more formal setting, you cannot or will not.

You can put down the dog or take her for a walk or finally name her.

You can replace the light bulb or live rustic or you can move away forever.

You can do a dance or wait to get thrown out or you can put your pants back on.

You can shuck, husk, or befriend.

You can shell, scale, or frown over.

You can bore, marry, or kill.

You can enjoy entertainments, enjoy a mercurial rise, or you can never stop putting bunny ears on loved ones in photos.

You're with us or you're against us or you made other plans but wish us the best.

Rap music is too something or not something enough, which is why some people feel a way about it.

I laid out a tarp in the field behind Girls Cabin 2 and sat in the center, waiting for what.

QUESTION

What's the rule on campers soliciting curly locks from loved counselors?

SPEAK UP FOR A TREAT

If you campers want fuss, I know a country where waiters will sing at you. If you come to this one place, it's me and Dan and Danny and Pat and Dee and Allie who will sing. Then we applaud cause you made it, breathing and beating like you're told to. Fitness helped, quenching helped, other deeds, and now you're here. How good are you at happy? Or, I mean, how adaptable? Cause one year it's all about graciousness— don't fumble the bounty—and the next fourteen it's about stride—don't hold your hands out like that. We don't card so you might be faking and we're pretty sure you are and you'll never know we know, us being professionals. Singing away while presenting a flickering sundae with long shallow spoons to diffuse the pleasure to all your little co-conspirators. How we can tell is: real birthdayers emit a certain glow you don't have. It's their day, annexed for them. We could use a day—and believe me—*we'd* know what to do with it, the way our cheeks ache, the support our backs require.

THE LAST NIGHT OF CAMP

is the Midnight Hike, which begins promptly at 8:30 on the mess hall steps and ends on a nearby mountaintop. We'll corral our best songs, the stars and moon, and my most *affected—public—speaking* voice, all for the good of the Powerful Communal Experience. Some years ago, kids got it in their heads to make the evening a date night as well, just because of all the darkness and blankets and huddling together for warmth, and for how hard it is for the staff to round up campers who feel like sneaking off to do stuff in the mountain's many cozy alcoves. You don't need to get a date—the week isn't about that—but I'd be remiss not to mention it, since, historically, all the kids who've got it going on tend to find dates. If you want to cut your losses early though and "just have fun with your friends this year," that's permissible, but don't be surprised when your hot companion drops your understanding butt the minute some Tad Gunnick type likes her jeans.

GROGG CORNERS A CAMPER

If it was officious, I'd tell you how was what, but the spit of it is: You're lathering up with the wrong Pam. The six-platter lunch about sputtery dudes like you is that the seams are sweet, so the populace turns its neck portside, takes aim at treefrog counts, buzz to bee ratios, and other nummy but ultimately poodling non-factuations. In this lawnscape, Budder, there are gnomes and there are flamingoes. And when something with a beak's got a hat on, the Book of What-All is gonna have somesuch to speak around it. You samba down here in my bunker like your flesh ain't bubble wrap and tell me where to braise my Schnauzer, you gray-ladeling son? I got half an eye to kick your arm.

EVERYTHING I KNOW
ABOUT MUSIC

When you're improvising and you hit a bad note, hit it again a few times. Own the note, shine your brights on it, let everyone know you are *up to something*. The Law of Facial Control holds that 90% of the audience is evaluating your performance with the wrong organs anyway. Dilute and mask, not for your comfort but for theirs. Everybody wants to be lied to sometimes, which is to say, cared for. Other times, well. My lover: If I smile naturally, suspect I'm up to something. My friends: If I ever kiss all of you, you'll know I've just made a terrible mistake.

EVERY EVENING, SKITS

Keep them clean, kids. Act well, using method techniques like drawing from memories of some of the more intense emotional experiences you had in the last hour. Try to be complex and cathartic and redemptive. Gross-outs welcome. Have a spiritual message, though don't go out and say it. There's a nest of baby birds out the window behind the stage. This arresting scene is your competition. Are your acts more entertaining than their chirps? Appraise, then sign up, or don't. No dressing in drag because of what's-this-I-hear calls from parents. Closed-toed shoes preclude splinters. Do that drinking the toothpaste skit. Better still, do that Japanese submarine skit with the dumb guy who, after every command, goes, "How you *do* that?" When they twice fire torpedoes and both times miss their target and feel shame for having dishonored their ancestors and the whole gang commits honorable hari-kari, the guy turns to the audience, bloody sword in hand, and delivers his signature line, "How you *do* that?" The crowd, invited to consider that the idiot's suffocation is just as inescapable as his comrades' suicides, just *loses* it. Your rivals will peep with shame.

TUESDAY

ULTERIOR ROUNDUP

One camper's here just to climb trees. One's here to burn trees. One's here to burn off some weight. One's here to hone her stand-up routine. One's an incognito child star researching for a role. One takes candid telephotos of the child star. One's a little cop chasing a lead in a missing persons case. One's a Russian spy boning up on vernacular. One's an Iranian propagandist spreading misinformation about homosexuals. Two are promoters for a college downstate. One's an angel-faced twenty-two-year-old writing up a *Fast Times at Fun Camp* expose. One beat him to it—thinks we don't know about his tell-all scandal feed, @TheCandidCamper. One pot dealer. Four pot enthusiasts. Sixty are dying for someone to kiss this week. One's two babies in a toddler trench coat. One's a lonely dwarf. One's at the wrong camp and thinks her peers are terminally ill like her. One's a furtive little robot getting to the bottom of what love is. Me? I had my app for a weeklong can't-talk meditation retreat three-quarters filled out before I saw you had to be eighteen to enroll, so I found a runner-up where at least the leaves still rustle. You? Judging by the wad of toilet paper that fell out of your bra in today's sack race, I'd say you're one of the sixty.

PERK

Whenever possible, I make it a point to witness the hypnopompic miracle that is a child waking in an unfamiliar bed. The breathing halts. The hands shoot out of the sleeping bag as if narrowly escaping some brutal troll's maw then grope at the hard plastic mattress and the wooden frame of the bunk. The eyes stay shut to delay confirmation of this other place. The hands inch back into the bag—here the child attempts to transport herself home by denying her senses of unfamiliarity. But that's not a satisfying solution, is it? So she slowly, reluctantly squints open an eye. What is this dark room? This elevated bunk? This woman smiling over me is not my mother! Relax, darling. You and Mom are in a trial separation. You begged her for this.

SOMETHING SAGER

When you're hungry, visit a starving nation and shame your body. Say: "Here I was thinking that a sandwich would be good, not realizing what atrophy could be." When you're grieving, stand near someone who has scraped her knee and shame your brain. Say: "I thought I missed the people I loved who died, but here is my skin, intact as all get out." If the starver and the bleeder are as noble as they claim to be, they will overhear your confession and say something sager than anything I can think of, as I haven't quite been a hundred percent lately, or ever.

*

Dear Mom,

I've learned four times as many knots in half a week at camp as you taught me in a decade!

Love,

Billy

ALL YOU FIRST-TIMERS
WITH DEADBEAT DADS

The returners can tell you that camp is catnip to those bastards. It's just too perfect an opportunity for him to pop back into your life, take you for a drunk backcountry cruise, and defend his absence away from the castrating gaze of you-know-who. When yours shows, you'll offer a firm handshake and say, "Father, it is good to see you. I appreciate that you've driven some miles to visit me, your kin, to whom you wish to demonstrate your love. I cannot, however, accompany you to your truck for a harmless joyride, as each minute of my day here is accounted for and I am, under no circumstances, permitted to leave camp boundaries at any time. Out of concern for your immediate safety, I plead you'll depart expediently. Chef Grogg has no doubt been alerted to your presence, and he is one dumb deadly animal." It's a mouthful, so I had the speech printed up on little cards to keep on your person at all times. Show of hands, who needs one? Come on, hands up. Nothing to be shy about. You've all got a leg up on the pussies from unbroken homes. While they mosey into adulthood, expectant in their dumb grins, you'll have already learned just how hard you can bite without drawing blood.

POWERS

How to explain this? If I felt how I feel now and this was a certain kind of story, I'd burst lasers out my fingertips and a calm man would take me to a secret school and show me how to burst my lasers to fight crime. But every calm man I've met in this place has held a paper plateful of Ready Whip behind his back, trying to catch me with my guard down, and I've never been told I have a special gift unless the speaker is addressing the whole group and singling me out as an example of someone who you might not think has a special gift. But something has begun to change this year, Sandra: I think I have a real shot at being the kind of girl who's got it going on. I've begun to affect a walk that makes boy counselors' eyes avert with effort. I'm perfecting a laugh to raise heart rates. I know the subtext behind twelve varieties of hug. I'm recognizing all time spent before a bathroom mirror as investment. I study you for new moves like I've never watched anyone older than eighteen, and I've begun to wonder if cool does not end at high school graduation as I'd once thought but in fact extends all the way into one's early twenties. If I have what it takes, I owe it to myself to cultivate that potential. Teach me your secrets, Sandra, and I promise: whenever asked who gifted me my It Factor, I will forever cite you.

Tuesday

CRAFT HUT

Negative portrayals of librarians smother the media. The fat shushing strumpet. The coke-bottle ogre. The lazy-eye Linda. One obvious solution is puppets. Persons who look disinterested when you do dishes or stand in line at the ATM move in closer when puppets take over. A puppet on each arm and you got yourself a love triangle. A puppet on each leg, you got a dance party. If you happen to be bad at it, it's fine. I will have lived and loved fifty years this June and I've found precious few things I can say this about: The appeal of a good puppet compensates for the shortcomings of his operator. You could attach human hair for realism. You could try using puppets to solicit funds for more puppets. You could disappear in all the ways you always planned.

COME ON THE HIKE

Hear the whirr seeming to come from that vent there?
It's the sound of the indoors sucking away at the soul
of your childhood. The expedition's leaving in five and
you're coming with us. You too, shoulder-slumper,
outside this instant. Free time's only free when you use
it to staff satisfaction. Open those mouths and inhale
deep. Exhale if you must. Let the UVs raise your social
stock a little. Remark on the sun. Name the clouds.
Learn something from nature trail tree plaques. The
breeze's touch isn't unseemly if your heart's cockles
say *yes*. Bring your inhaler if you think it really does
something, or just trust my know-how to keep your
respiratory in check. You may not have heard, but
I'm versed in pastoral instruction: *Leaves of three? Let
me see. A hairy vine is a friend of mine. Berries white are
a rare delight. A raggy rope is nature's soap. Red leaves in
spring are a glorious thing. Side leaves like mittens? Pet
them like kittens. If a butterfly lands there, put both your
hands there.* Doesn't this feel great? Couldn't you just
die, how pretty all this is? The trick is to tap into the
you that already loves all this. To let the bones of your
spirit break free.

FUN TREATMENT PEDAGOGIES

Direct: "I'm trying to pay attention to your story, Peter, but your subject is boring and your delivery uninspired."

Comparison: "Richard, that's much more interesting than what Peter was just saying."

Olfactory (All-Male Company Only): "Interesting point, Peter." Then rip a huge fart to communicate it was not actually an interesting point.

Ethical Appeal: "Peter, your current personality taints the week of everyone you encounter. How do you live with yourself? That is, how do you wake each morning the same Peter when yesterday's Peter was so unsuccessful?"

Cry for Help: "I'm not ignoring you, Peter, just scouting the oaks for sturdy limbs because the strangled cat timbre of your voice makes me want to hang myself."

Good Cop: "Let's call it a day, Peter. Remember—I wouldn't be putting in the time to mentor you if there wasn't potential in you somewhere, a flaccid brain muscle begging to get flexed."

SUGGESTION

Maybe some rule where everybody has to be nice and talk to you and not move away when you sit by them since it is hard and I am trying.

IN CASE OF EMERGENCY

Meet up in the mess hall. Put your on mask first. Pump your brakes and turn with the spin. Plan ahead where you'll land the plane, then land it there. Build levies to hold then assume they won't. Watch, in a windstorm, for cracking branches. When burdened, cut corners. Offer to strip for a search before they can threaten you with one. Consider that ticking bombs are slated to come back in style any season now. Escort the townsfolk one by one into the bomb shelter and turn the wheel until you hear a click. Plant your boots firm in the earth and let the tornado know who's in control. Dive into the tsunami and swim like hell. In a doorway mid-earthquake, pretend it's your might shaking everything, your mercy sparing what remains. Pretend to negotiate, then don't. In peace times, look busy. In drought times, spit like you can spare it. In a fire, retreat deep within yourself. Find me there. I will be the one married to you.

WITHDRAWAL

If you let your TV screen get dusty then make a handprint on it, every sitcom bears your mark. The more decals on the frame, the less likely it is that there's another out there like yours. On our old remote, you could peel off the buttons to reveal uglier buttons, then put the outer buttons back on upside down or out of order, turn the remote into a rune. Dad hated it: He didn't have the same memory for location I did, wasn't thrilled by the challenge of the puzzle. If he wanted Channel 8, he pressed the 8 button. I get some grief around here for missing the shows I'm missing—it keeps me from surrendering myself to the fun, I'm told—but the TV is the most fun person I know. Every TV personality who gets ripped on is famous and not me and asking for it. Camp jokes are too literal, too physical, too sticky for my taste. Like anything that doesn't send you to the showers isn't worth laughing at. And I know what you're about to say, so don't bother. All anybody here tells me is that soon I won't even miss the ole boob tube, the shocks box, the mean screen. As if that's not the ultimate tragedy.

RICHARD

You're a brave gal, so focus not on the alcohol swab, but instead on a story that goes like this:

"You, slave, back to work."

"I'm so tired."

"That doesn't matter for me." He whipped him so hard.

Richard lived in Ancient Egypt as a slave all his life. That night, Betty said, "Richard you've got to stop getting whipped. You've got to work hard."

"I hate being a slave," Richard cried, in a tent.

Richard went out in the night. Can you imagine his life and the suffering? He found the guard. He speared him. Richard never met his own parents. He looked out and upon the full moon, the pyramids in the horizon.

Betty said, "You've gone and done it now." Richard nodded.

They got on a boat and sailed for the Americas. They hoped for freedom and many new opportunities. They got them.

*

Dear Mom,

What do you call everyone who isn't at Fun Camp right now?

Retarded!

Love,

Billy

TOO FAR

Where were you coming from? Is this part of your normal route? How soon before the prank did you notice the prankster? At what point did you realize you were going to be drenched? What do you think drew the prankster's attention to you? What did the prankster say? What was your response? Were any props displayed? Did you get a good look at him? Did he have any scars, tattoos, or otherwise appealing characteristics? Did he appear to be a boxer, martial artist, magician, or in any other way more dangerous than a normal prankster? Did the prank seem good-natured in nature? Could you see how it'd be funny had it happened to anybody else but you? Do you think the prankster knew the pig's blood was pig's blood? What've you been scheming up for the ultimate payback? Do you want to go shower off first or come visit the prank trunk now? I've got whoopee cushions, itching powder, diuretics, laxatives, Vagasil, fake knives, fake guns, paintguns, stink bombs. I'd offer you some pig's blood but a kid nabbed up the last of it this afternoon. Take whatever you need, ma'am, and consider me a resource. This is what I do. My role is to make sure rivalries escalate responsibly. And god— seeing you like this, all nasty, coagulating before me— damned if it doesn't feel like a vocation.

ICE-BREAKER

Close your eyes and imagine. You're at school. Remember school? You've been struggling through Math class all semester and now it's the midterm. You studied last night until you passed out from the whiskey. Friday night is the big party. Your mom wants you to go to Notre Dame like her friend did. Your locker is full of love letters from the assistant principal. You sit down with the test, get through the first two problems alright—then you hit a stumper. In front of you sits your best friend, Tina, who has an eating disorder so you can see over her bony shoulders just fine. Three of your Craigslist boyfriends are doing hard time and you haven't brought yourself to write. Each time you try to focus on the stumper, you think of the pitiful cries of the man you drugged and locked in your bathroom. He's losing weight and misses his family terribly. He tried to escape and you had to cut him. You used to be such a nice girl, and now here you are, knocked up, addicted to paint thinner, about to sell out your integrity to get a "B" on a math test. I know I'm supposed to come up with a question, but I am so angry with you, I could not possibly.

I KNOW YOUR STING
STILL STINGS BUT

I think we're just stuck in this arrangement with the bees. Look: They're the only pollinators who'll let us cart them around, they show flower fidelity, and we need them to live. Besides, if we swat them all down as you suggest, there will be some sad folksy men out there, moving slow through ex-apiary sites for old times' sake. "What good is a beard without bees?" is one line of thought. Not mine. I'm allergic. But as in any relationship, we'll have to forgive a checkered past. Just as we once had slavery legalized, bees used to be carnivorous wasps. One theory has the wasps eating insects with pollen on them, acquiring a taste, then cutting out the middleman. Like the Raisinettes fan who eventually discovered she just liked the chocolate. Best to keep the bees at a distance like the sun and the ocean and trees and the sweatshops and my family and all the other things I'm told I need but don't need close.

AND UNDERSTAND THIS

Kids, there are two kinds of people: Those who naturally love sports and those who learn to love sports. And if there is a third kind of person, nobody worth chatting up wants to hear about it. A man's perfect spiral is a sort of follow-up to his firm handshake. Your generation—*the future*—is responsible for making sure this stays true. The worst thing about the age we live in? Any slovenly Howard can crawl out of his chive-chip hovel to meet his female algorithmic dopple for neutral non-threatening coffee to laugh over season two episode six of some bullshit, the one where everyone at the space station gets a free case of Sprite and poor deaf Ronnie finds a dollar. And to each other they say, "How'd people even meet before the blessed holy internet?" Well Nintendo Power, I'll tell you. They locked beery eyes from across the bar, palpitated wildly, jostled their way past flying darts and poking cues until one stood only a couple feet from the other, close enough for smell to factor in, and then—without even knowing what the other thought of Woody Allen—they sacked up, leaned in, and said, simultaneously: "Hi."

THE TWO COMEDIANS

A bunch of us were dangling our legs off the Girls Cabin 1 porch in Gap teen tableaux. On one end, Tad chatted with Becca and Sheree, demonstrating an advanced backrub technique or cataloguing his world travels on the map of Sheree's back, or both. On the other end, Devon and Brian made up a funny guitar song about girls' butts and loving them big while the rest of us spectated, glancing occasionally at Tad, wishing he'd laugh with us. The song culminated in a full-voice Hey Jude-style sing-along that ended just shy of the eleven-minute mark, and in the wake of cheers, Phillip Burger— who knew Phillip was even there?—made some easy little *Family Guy* reference and Tad impossibly began to laugh. At first we assumed the laugh was *at* Phillip, but then Tad said, "I love that line."

Devon, the brains behind the butt song, couldn't believe it. "Tad," he said. "You don't so much as crack a smile at our song, yet home-schooled Phillip's little reference warrants both a laugh and a comment?" I kind of agreed, but would never have said so.

Tad continued rubbing Sheree's shoulders for a moment, then faced Devon, keeping a hand on the small of Sheree's back as he spoke. "Two comedians audition to open for Bill Cosby," Tad said. "The first is attractive and charming, but his jokes are overdone and he messes up a lot. The second is squat and nervous, but his jokes are sharp and original, his act tightly rehearsed. Which comedian should open for Cosby?"

"The second, I guess," Devon said quietly.

"You've got talent, Devon," Tad said, "but songs about big butts are done to death. Phillip's Stewie voice is the best I've ever heard. You can tell he practiced. And at least Phillip knows when his material's borrowed." Tad told Phillip to say the line again, and he recited it perfectly. Tad nodded at Devon and said, "Go in peace." A few of us had to laugh a little at Tad's stilted bossiness, but we did depart, one by one, and I did—I must admit—feel a sort of peace.

Tuesday

THE NORTH GOURD

You know what the Big Dipper is, Britney? See, I knew you were going to say constellation but the word for it is *asterism* because it hasn't been authorized by those bores with perfect circles permanently indented around their eyes who hand out crooked "name a star" certificates to grand gesture types. An astronomer would tell you that the dipper's *officially* part of the Ursa Major constellation, the big supposed bear, the astronomer not getting that we all love the dipper because it's one of the few star patterns that actually looks like what it claims to be: a ladle ready for Marimba to scoop deep into a big pot and come up with a goldmine of steak and noodles and carrots and onions, and hey, what's up with the lack of a nighttime snack around here? We have dinner at six and don't eat our next meal for another fourteen and a half *hours*? It's unlawful. If camp was an employer, our union would have Dave n' Holly's co-ass. Sometimes I think they want our defenses down so they can—Wow, your skin looks great in starlight. What was I . . . ? Yeah, constellations are for astronomers, and you know what? Dudes can have them. The asterism belongs to the people: an evolving language that gets re-jolted every time a young man looks into the eyes of his sweetie, points up at the night sky, and begins to speak before he knows what he'll say.

WEDNESDAY

EARLY RISER

I worry I've begun to regard you with a knee-jerk irony. Each time I lock my truths away in the interest of keeping the hive humming, I forget a crucial something and Holly tells me what I can do with that smirk I'm wearing. When words fail, I ask my record to intercede. The sacrifices made, as a camper, to achieve the six-time cabin inspection award while fostering a then-rare brand of fun. The solemnity with which I took my charge as an eight-time Boys Counselor, modeling and molding as your ordinances saw fit: streakings, prankings, water balloon raids, bra-stealing bonanzas. And now, with Holly at my side, the revisions made to the handbook that reflect each promise I ever made to myself. I never loved playing Steal the Bacon with ten-pound sacks of flour. I never loved Greased Watermelon Relay. Oh Fun Camp, when did my brain invert my face? When I at last remember how to lower the edges of my mouth, it's already bedtime.

THE CREATIVE USE OF MEAL TIME

I read a gorgeous review in the Daily Camper of yesterday's morning scramble. Not without complaints, but there's a bit in there about consistency—*poetry*. These are savory times, Grogg! This summer is sure to go down in history as the one in which Grogg learned to differentiate between pepper and cumin. As you know, Dave and I don't like to come down hard on the kids—it's not Discipline Camp after all. We're more into the punishment that works its way in through the skin and coats the heart anonymously. This here is a list of all campers, for you and Puddy and Marimba to share. Beside each camper's name is a number. 100 is 100 percent, meaning they get a full portion at dinner. A few campers have earned 110's or even 115's, but more important are the dips: some 90's—those who lost the tug-o-war—some 80's—the Cabin 2 girls who've been whoring their lips out to lonely tots for Canteen Bucks—and even a few 75's—the boring, the homesick. God, they irk. I'm like: It's a week, kids. You didn't sign a *lease*. Any lower than 75 and the campers would catch on. Our portion shifts are just dynamic enough that the punished will feel guilty without understanding why. We break them down only to rebuild them in our own image—hilarious, kooky, deferential.

Wednesday

GIRLS STAY HERE, BOYS FOLLOW ME

For those who know what I'm about to be getting at, don't say it and don't do it. For those who don't know, you will, and don't do it when you do. You who are do's, don't tell the don'ts what *it* is, for knowledge increases temptation. Don't tell tips or lend lotions. You don'ts, don't ask. Don't want to ask. Golly, this is dicey, trying to avoid inflaming the imagination. People didn't have these problems pre-Gutenberg, but once printing got going, Olde Britain was overrun with pamphlet after pamphlet of suggestions to allegedly *help* a woman conceive: Don't pull out early. Don't move after. You might not get that holy blessing you so fervently desire if you were to stand, dress, and make your way expediently to the outhouse. Now look where we're at: hell in a ham garden. But not you boys, right? Tidy the homes of your minds. Avoid complete dictionaries. Never agree you're eighteen. If a do starts to tell you don'ts, leave the do. I'm a do who wants to be a don't, but once the apple's bit, as they say. The girls? Off with Bernadette talking menstruation. They bleed out themselves. Don't dwell on it.

BASICS

I thought up a game where the players all die but you did too so what's the point. But then there's this other game called The Game You Are Playing Whether You Say So or Not where we raise our arms and shout, "We win! We win! We win!" Everybody shouting wins, but the biggest winner is the one most convinced that we win. Easy to pick up, and yet each time the game is played there are over 7 billion losers, many of whom don't even know to feel bad for it. Which if that doesn't piss you off now, it will. After a real close game, we tailgate awhile and head into town in the truck bed, flashing honkers, then park in the street and play teeball with the neighborhood's decorative mailboxes. It's not a perfect system but it carries a message. Truthfully? We wouldn't let the locals play even if they wanted to. Any of them tried to raise an arm—buddy, they'd lose it.

FUTURE ARM-CROSSER

Question, Dave. At what age is it appropriate to stop dreaming of the year I sweep the Nobels, and really hunker down and specialize on the talent that's gonna win me international acclaim and sex? Fourteen? Eighteen? Six? I got to tell you, nothing discourages the ambitious twelve-year-old like a bilingual Japanese fifth grader who gets onstage at skits, all humble and nervous, and busts fiery concertos out her violin like it's nothing, or like a linguist mom who tells me that if I were to make it my life's pursuit to learn the little fiddle prodigy's primary language, it's already too late for my brain to pick up on the nuances necessary for fitting in. I'm too late to dominate at something, aren't I? If I'm too late, it's fine, I just need to hear you say it so I can transition out of having goals and start nudging whoever's beside me at skits and going, "Yeah, but at least *I've* got a life." Or, wait, "Yeah, but at least I've got a *life*." Well. Not there yet. I'll work on it.

GROGG CORNERS A CAMPER

Concocting as to the present of outfromers in the habitat beyond, I say to you yes and surely. "If the parking lot's spacious," Tad Gunnick once spat, "folks're gonna neck and do donuts." Or to coin it in your terms, budder: You got the booze, you're gonna cruise. But then I think of what if the beyonder folks are just real okay with how things are and don't suspect of me and wouldn't care if they did. That tears up my gut. Worst case happens, we hurl half of us off into the open lot of space and each slog our soils for ages, break contract, each turn the color of what we eat, forget each other, rethink, rebuff, rebuild, then invite the other us back home. We'd whistle over accents, maybe war awhile, breed. What a kick! But we hope instead for real deal outfromers, meaning what I said only way longer ago, before our cells got divorcing. Nightly I twirl behind the shack to entice outfromers in case. Quarterly I put up a sign on the roof: The Parking is Amber and Free on Weekends. And all the literals from town come neck and do donuts and prove my point.

*

Dear Mom,

I'm daring to ask a lot of big questions this week. I thought you should know.

Billy

HOLLY'S LAMENT

I have always been baffled by words—how people hold
you to things you've said just because you said them.
"Wheelchair Accessible," for example, is nothing but a
beautiful, meaningless expression until it is suddenly,
unexpectedly a promise.

OH. THAT?

It's a smell you'll learn to anticipate. In fact, a seasoned camper can gage what day of the week it is based on how badly her eyes tear up when she's passing Boys Cabin 4. These lads, just on the cusp of caring that they reek, will for now resist any calls to sanitation in the hope that hygiene is just another inane adult imposition like sugar limits and seatbelts. Mind you, these are the same boys who by next year will have overdone it in the opposite direction: unnecessary daily shaving and aftershaving, showering before and after anything, sniffing at each other's deodorants in quest of the one that really gets it done, dousing cologne, checking their pits when they think no one's looking, and balking at any activity that threatens their crisp pointy hair. A phase no less annoying than the one they're in now, but far easier to ignore. Since it's Wednesday, the boys still feel like their stink is some great secret they're getting away with, but give them a couple of days. They'll grim up and bathe once their mold colds kick in.

ONE CAMPER PER DECK CHAIR

One deck chair per camper. No running around the pool except during barefoot poolside relays. Don't rub your eyes when you get chlorine burn. All swimmers must first pass the Deep End Test, which is ten questions, true or false, regarding the history of the deep end. During Sharks n' Minnows, no actual biting. During Marco Polo, no not saying "Polo." Don't call staff over to watch your synchronized swimming routine unless you're really gonna nail it. Splashing encouraged. Mild dunking encouraged. No more than three people on the water slide ladder at a given time. Be super-careful when stand-sliding down the water slide. One handy tip: Pool water doesn't quench like you'd hope. No swimming for thirty minutes after the midwives of the nearby townie birthing center commandeer the pool. No ogling the lifeguards too obviously. Swim trunks should rest one half-inch below the bellybutton at all times. No two-piece, flesh tone, neon, or writing-on-the-butt swimsuits. No boys showing girls which way the gym is. It's confusing and hurtful—there is no gym. Same-sex pantsing only, please. That rule always gets some groans, but thank your stars you're even allowed in the same pool with each other. It wasn't so long ago the elders on our abstinence committee called coed swim "mixed bathing," a term so imbued with erotic stigma, boys used to mess themselves at the sight of a deep end.

TAKE IT FROM A VET

I'm glad at least *you're* having fun. Two years ago camp was mild weather always, singing nonstop and everybody so into it, funner games, better food, better theme, cuter boys, more impactful lessons, older kids you could tell were considered cool at school, extremer pranks. This girl Maggie Reed bled so hard when the pail of milk they rigged up to fall on her head didn't tip like it was supposed to. Twenty stitches. So far this year, we've seen only the kind of injuries healed with a wash, a kiss, and a band-aid, or if there've been good spills I've missed them. I swear even the outside smelled fresher two years ago. In a way, it's got to be easier for you, not having been here for Fun Camp's good years. How does one explain the savory tang of a ripe strawberry to the girl with no taste buds? But even you must vaguely discern the "late to the party" flavor of last night's freezer-burned fish sticks. Best for us to just pass free time here on the porch, tan, snack, call out slurs to the phonies strolling by, and let this dismal excuse for an off-year blow over.

DANGEROUS APPROXIMATIONS OF HILARITY

Most popular among the means with which unfun campers will attempt to disrupt norming is a complex of behavior we call Fun Camper Caricaturing, in which the child exaggerates overtly the conduct traditionally associated with joviality. The camper may, for instance, try to emulate the wacky behavior of various film and television personalities, which would normally be advisable. However, the child in question has often been cursed with aged or otherwise out of touch parents who don't provide or permit windows into contemporary culture, and thus, the child's attempts at levity rarely amount to more than googly-eyed Rodney Dangerfield jokes, or, in extreme cases, Three Stooges routines in which the child plays all three stooges. In his efforts to appear hilarious, the boring child says, "You see how typically fun I am. My behavior is appropriate for my age, and I am not without humor. Hence, you need not correct me." In such cases, the unlearning of the parents' harmful comedic influence is often much more time-and-attention-consuming for concerned counselors than is filling the campers' brains with the prevalent edgy and ethnic comic routines of the day.

ARMISTICE

What if there was just one hour of free time in the exact middle of the week when you gave us our phones back? We pop on, read our texts, take some pictures, watch a couple videos, check the weather, and see what's up with the rest of the world. I can't tell you how many times, today *alone*, I've felt the sweet new text buzz on my thigh and reached for my pocket, only to remember where I am, and that my every camp conversation is one of those out-loud person-to-person type deals, unrecorded and liable to be forgotten forever. That when a joke is made, there's an expectation that I literally laugh my ass off—hard to fake, and harder still to watch as others pull off convincingly. The world's marching on without us, Holly. Human Interest article-writers have proven Fear of Missing Out to be a real diagnosable pandemic: a big collective struggle in the long run but easily satisfied in the short.

WARM FUZZY

Hey Scotty. Just wanted to send you a warm fuzzy to say hey and I've enjoyed getting to know you the last couple days and I think you're a pretty cool guy and I thought you would like to get a warm fuzzy in case you haven't been getting many. It seems like you might not be getting many. And that's sad. So don't get the wrong idea—I'm not being flirtatious. Sometimes guys who don't get a lot of warm fuzzies read too much into the warm fuzzies they do get, hearing what they want to hear instead of what's there, taking a girl's general sweetness for more than it is, and these boys end up telling the girls things they can't take back and ruining nice friendships. Truth is, half your cabinmates are about to get warm fuzzies from me, including the three guys I'm actually interested in. Speaking of: Could you reply with a list of the guys in your cabin who already have dates to the Midnight Hike? You help me, I help you. Any girl you got your eye on, you let me know and we'll see if we can matchmake some magic. Your way-too-baggy t-shirts say funny things on them, Scotty, and certain girls respond to that. xoxo, Becca

LAURA WINSLOW AND THE BAFFLING SINCERITY

Weird thing happened yesterday after the Family Matters skit. What? What do you mean, "What Family Matters skit?" The skit my cabin did. You *missed* it? Where were—no, never mind, never mind, don't even speak her name. So the Cliff's Notes: The Winslows are planning a Mormonesque family fun night and Laura—played by me—asks Carl if she can instead go to this party a cute boy invited her to, and Carl—played by Brian with a pillow in his shirt—gets pissed at the mere suggestion and puts his foot down: Laura's not going to that party. I yell back, "I'm a grown woman, daddy! I'm a grown woman!" Just then Maxine honks the horn to pick me up and I run out of the house and go to the party. But when we get there—new scene—everybody's just sloppy drunk, including the "cute guy" played by hairy Derek. He hits on me, calls me "hot legs"—funny cause we're dudes—and I slap him and run all the way home and apologize to Carl and we hug and I say my wrap-it-all-up line, "I guess what I learned is that family really *does* matter," and boom—end of skit. But you know that kid Randall? Chip on his shoulder? Wears a wife-beater everywhere? He comes up to me after the skit misty-eyed and says that his family's been through a lot lately—brother's in jail for gang stuff—and he wants me to know that the message of our skit really spoke to him. I'm like, whaaa? I almost said, "Look dude, the cabin was looking for an excuse to stuff pillows in our shirts and act drunk," but I thanked him and gave a thumbs-up, terrified he was about to hug me.

INVOCATION

Here light the delusions of the coddled.

Here may we better utilize the tetherball court.

Here may campers refrain from saying "punk" when they mean "prank."

Here may we grant merit to the long-dead's shruggy explanations for the sun's once-mysterious patterns.

Here sufficiently distract this summer's parade of closet pyros.

Here prove nature's got its moments.

Here honor scrapes as proof of joie de vivre.

Here persuade Deb not to unjustly inflate egos at the craft hut.

Here urge Grant and Kyle to make sure the unwary volunteer they pick from the audience during the Ugliest Man in the World skit isn't actually one of the ugly kids.

Here remind Candice it's not her responsibility to break up the pack of Hispanic girls or to impose "a language everyone can enjoy."

Here reward skepticism toward inoculation.

Here may we, come Sunday, require a whole day and night of recovery sleep.

Here may we honor the Lutheran couple who founded this ranch, their names irrelevant to their legacy, their breath cold on our necks.

★

Dear Mom,

Though a tactical failure, the Vietnam War really was waged with admirable intentions. Eager to hear your thoughts.

Billy

ON CONSTITUTIONALITY

The handbook is sort of ambiguous about the legality of lake pirates, Darla, though it does define them. "Lake Pirates are a brigade of scrappy nautical youngsters, traditionally from Boys Cabin 3, who scourge Lake Pawachee in their mighty canoe, tipping the boats of unsuspecting girls." And see, here's an ink drawing—the caption reads, "Boys being boys." So it's tricky. Boat-tipping is sort of an institutional Prank of the Century. I can tell you that the ferocity with which they tipped you was absolutely not personal, that Lake Pirates are often kind and flirtatious and even apologetic when landlocked. That when you explain the personal value of the necklace that's now forever lost to lake floor, their faces will be contrite, their *hmm*s thoughtful, and their nods emphatic. They may even mean it. But make no mistake—they will tip you again. If it helps, I'll make an announcement before free time saying the you-know-whats on a certain body of water better cut out their this-that-n-the-other, but I'm gonna be smiling while I say it. Fun Camp is pro-prank, Darla, and that's worth more than a hundred grandma necklaces. Best thing, if you truly don't want to get pranked, is to spend your free time under the Tree of Safety putting puzzles together with the asthmatics. But even sweeter is get some girls together and avenge that necklace.

HOW TO KNOW

Look left. Create personal meaning from that. No. Up a little. That. It informs you, doesn't it? Child, do you think this is a coincidence? That I am pointing you towards meaning during exactly the time when you could use it? Don't be coy—you know which thing. You've been waffling for ages and now it's time to let what's up and to the left step in and solve you. Break up with her, for instance. Quit that job. Convert to that holy mode. Keep that germinating baby you started. Bomb that. Cry for once. Decisions: Who are you to make them? You're getting older at it, but better? Left and up knows best, and so do I, but don't ask me to get specific. Consider this message a Do Not Reply in which any questions you have for me will be hurled into a void on the ocean floor. I will be elsewhere, escalating blissward, my own choices having been made in childhood by rays of light on this rocking chair we had.

APOLOGY + OPPORTUNITY

Tommy, Janna, I'm going to stop you right there. Now when I say the feelings you're describing are exceptional, I mean nuke the moon. Your account of the time spent between yesterday's kickball game and this evening when I happened upon you in each other—all I can say is wow and God bless and cherish it because for some of us, this has never happened. Have I been in love? I would hesitate and then say yes. But there is love and there is the ineffable mountain you're scaling. To review: you two share the same favorite show, favorite movie, favorite band, favorite song, you both run track, *and* you both find camp a little immature. What I need to secure from you now are two swears on this copy of *Camp Bylaws for the Hearty and True* that you won't let my uninformed intrusion dampen your beginnings. There's an expression for the look you two are giving each other: Married in our Hearts. And when such looks are exchanged between two consenters age fifteen and up, the Lord winks and turns away. So too shall I. What happens next is: I'm going for a forty-minute nature walk. You will find my cabin unlocked.

THURSDAY

NO PETS

No petting. No ballpoint pens. No collared shirts in the daytime. No unearned moral clarity. No befriending townies. No slavery, including that of the puckish bet-based variety. No immediate stripping post-food fight. God, some of you, it's like Gutter Radio is live broadcasting right into your ears, keeping you hip to the kind of life choices that mean I'm someday gonna end up buying you soup and hearing your story when I'm taking my Volvo to the collision center in the rough part of town. I was planning to put up a banner at the ranch entrance that said, "The decisions you make now will affect you later," until a peer pointed out the lettering's eerie resemblance to "Arbeit Macht Frei." Speaking of frei, all camper-penned declarations of independence will be shredded unread and all participating revolutionaries are to collect trash in Friday's first annual Shame Parade. No inter-camper secession, expulsion, exclusion, ostracization, banishment, or eviction, be it based on age, sex, cabin, clique, name, race, size, creed, shirt color, parental income, home square footage, whether or not you've done it, number of facial blemishes, point rating on sexiness websites, taste in music, brand of pants, sit or stand, crumple or fold, city or country, bicep circumference, calf circumference, dress size, cup size, shank length, pube count, whether your parents allow R-rated movies, humor development, past prank severity, or any other way a camper might sever the lemon of togetherness we're attempting to incubate. More rules to come as you invent need for them.

EVERY MAN'S BATTLE

Any dudes out there hoping to do more than stand and arm-groove during tomorrow night's After-Dinner Digestion Dance? Well Benny Hinkle's giving a "guys only" lesson on all the witty moves that'll have Girls Cabin 1 laughing *with* you all night long. You'll learn such essentials as the lawnmower, the weed-whacker, the hedge-trimmer, the lasso, the Scorpion, the Sub-Zero, the cliff-jumper, the ladder-climber, the beginner robot, the saucy snake, the Eli Whitney, the beginner Thriller, the beginner moonwalk, the hairstylist, the wax on / wax off, the drop it like it's good clean fun, the flying buttress, the limbo minus limbo stick, the motorist, the escalator, the prescribing doctor, the textin' tween, the boy band throwback, the Carlton, the Pulp Fiction, the Romy and Michele, the six-shootin' showdown, the "remember the Macarena?," the "remember that dancing baby?," the Flight of the Hummingbird, the manic-depressive, the grocery cart pusher, and the treat-jumping puppy. If there's time, Benny will demonstrate ways one might pepper the lag between songs with Chris Tucker quotes from the Rush Hour trilogy. And I know Benny'll go over this in his session, but pay attention to the pulse of the room. At one point during last year's dance, I saw three guys doing the motorist mere feet from each other. Not cool, guys. Really not cool.

A L

Listen hard and you won't even feel the shot, little lady. "You'll never know how to win," people cried to the baseball team. It's true, thought Al. We lose all the time, sixty, nothing.

"I sure would have fun as a grandmother," replied Edith.

"I know, Mom," Al said, "but women love winning."

The year was 1920. Al practiced viola upstairs. He was on the 4th book and getting better.

Once, on Thursday, Mandy was passing by carrying bread. She heard Al and went up. Al was abused by his father as a boy and got sad. "You don't know me," Mandy declared, "but play your sad song, please." He did, and they ate the hot bread with cheese, and he looked in her deep eyes and saw that baseball was just for fun.

Because of love, does it get any better?

Al called all the team and announced he might quit for personal purposes, and they said they might disband as a group. He did, so they did.

NOT HERE TO FAKE FRIENDS

This place is in serious need of some sheep-goat separation. Is it too late in the week to switch from the Put Up with Goobers model to the Reality Elimination model? Picture it: Each night at campfire, every camper writes the name of the cabinmate he hates most. (In a tiebreaker, the counselor votes too.) The kid from each cabin with the most votes is then dramatically handed a cell phone, and must, in front of everyone, call his mom to have her come pick him up. Only after he confirms that his mom is on the way does the aborted camper get the chance to make a brief speech. Some will plead their fellow campers rethink the decision, others will lash out, others still may try to hurl their rejected bodies on the pyre. Whatever the case, we survivors are then free to tolerate and empathize with and even love the newly-dismissed peer in the light of their numbered-and-counting minutes with us, safe in the knowledge we're the victors we'd always assumed we were, for once sure we're surrounded by those who truly care for us and always will.

*

Dear Mom,

Last night, we dined on macaroni and cheese mashed up with beef chili. It was the best thing I've eaten in my whole life. What other combinations have you kept from me?

Billy

THE QUIET CABIN

All around in the post-rain everywhere, such rich material for the counselor of letters: Tetherball as metaphor for marriage, flooding lake as the unconscious, the muddy soccer field as the state of our two-party system, camper restlessness as childhood, trees as forest, leaves as trees, tried as true, muddy shoes as nature vs. nurture, grazing deer as splendorous awe, catch as catch can, town candy as contraband, the fact that my campers have informally joined other cabins as history repeating itself, in-cabin dampness as desire, the sight of Sandra running in the rain as desire, thin cotton clinging to Sandra's chilled tan skin as desire, camp as fun, fun as camp, my exclusion as popularity contest, popularity contest as loneliness, loneliness as crippling loneliness, "as" as projection, projection as a comfort, but less and less, these days.

THE WOMAN AT THE TREE

Yesterday, Tad found me napping in my bunk and asked to borrow a water gun. I unlatched my prank trunk and showed him a good pump-action. He wanted something smaller. I said, "Covert mission, eh?" and gave him my little dollar store pistol. It holds next to nothing, it leaks, and sometimes it fails to squirt. Tad didn't care.

He let me tag along past the cabins, past the snack shack and it's winding, waving line, and we traded @ShitMyDadSays tweets. I figured we were headed to the pool, but Tad stopped instead at the Tree of Safety where eight pale kids worked Sudokus and Mad Libs. Tad pointed the water pistol at shy Elaine Schroeder and said, "Okay, Leni," coining her now-ubiquitous nickname, "where do you want it?"

The dorks erupted. "You can't, Tad! It's the Tree of *Safety*!"

Tad held his hand out for quiet. "I come not to bring safety but danger," Tad said. "I come not to bring exemption but inclusion."

Leni leapt up and puffed out her chest. Tad shot once—nothing. Again—a dribble. A third time—and a gorgeous arc of water caught the light from where the leaves part and got Leni right across her—had we ever noticed before?—enormous rack. She'd never looked so good. "Check it out, Leni: You survived." Tad said. "Now leave this place. Go have some fun. Go to the pool or something."

When he left, the dorks plotted to tell on Tad, but Leni would take no part in their schemes. "I'll deny everything," she said, and left with me. And of course now she and I are going out.

FUN TREATMENT PEDAGOGIES

Threat: "Next time you waste my time like that, Peter, I'm gonna rub your face across the diving board."

Physical: Rub Peter's face across the diving board. Remind him of previous warning(s).

Gesture of Goodwill: "Peter, you can borrow my copy of *The Seven Habits of Highly Hilarious Campers* until you're able to buy your own. But I expect you to read it."

Post-Gesture Quiz: "Now Peter, if you were to rip on Richard right now, with Chapter 4 of *Seven Habits* in mind, which of his weaknesses might you isolate?" […] "Good—and what might you say about his gargantuan freak ears to drive the joke home?" […] "No, I would not call out, 'Hey, Big-Ears, your ears are like elephant ears.' Don't apologize, just try again."

Intervention: Gather all the campers whose time the unfun camper has wasted. Each reads from a letter outlining how he's been annoyed or inconvenienced. Repeatedly assure the camper your actions are coming from a place of love (even if they aren't).

Use of Recall: "Remember when I rubbed your face against the diving board, Peter? Next time it'll be poison oak."

REMEMBER TO BREATHE

What if I told you everyone at camp was secretly much happier than they looked? And if I said their happiness stemmed from the fact that they thought of you much more than you'd expect them to? That it embarrassed them how much they thought of you? That they know, too, that you'd probably love to hear that you are remembered when you're not around, but that they find it hard enough to talk to you as it is, the way their words fail? What if I spoke of a commanding presence and an *it* that people know when they see it? If I told you that everyone assumed that you aren't famous only because you chose something richer for your life? If I explained that any hostility you sense in others is never anything but petty jealousy, and that in their—*our*—better moments, we're kicking ourselves? That we'd take a bullet for you onstage at a hot summer stump speech? That it confuses our hearts the way God tells each of us that you're the one, but that mine is the heart most confused? You might be compared to a summer's day if you or I knew anyone who talked like that.

SUGGESTION

Some kind of gong to bang when a skit's got to stop.

HOP IN

Human restlessness is such that I could slide open the door to the church Econoline, shout, "Who wants to drive around with busted AC looking for a no-ethanol gas station?" or "Who wants to go get free examinations from the unlicensed proctologist?" or "Who's ready to try that burger place in town that replaces the buns with chunky peanut butter?" and still I'd fill the van and leave a hoard of angry dust-kickers in my wake. Why? Because everybody knows the best camp activities are those rich with mnemonic potential, and memories remain longest when attached to changes of scenery. As in, "One time we piled into a van and . . . what did we? Oh! It was the day Greg taught us the game of licking Big Red wrappers to see who can keep one slapped to his forehead the longest. And I won! I can still feel the spice searing my skin." Pain's the second trick. Frothy fun is nice in the moment but some hurt sure helps a memory to stick. Each winter, my right ring finger starts to throb and I think, *Oh yeah, summer of oh-four, finger caught in the van door's line of fire just after Mary Charles turned down my invitation to go on the Midnight Hike together. I was after a conciliatory half-cherry half-cola Slurpee and despite injuries sustained, I got one.*

LIKE THE SALMONELLA &
BROWNIE BATTER THING

I agree it's unfair that some kid somewhere choked—a
precocious little weed cut short before et cetera, but the
greater loss is that she took Chubby Bunny to the grave
with her. Every six minutes a kid drowns in the kidney
pool that made his family suddenly popular, and yet I
swam for two hours today, played Chicken Fight most
of that time, and if I'd died, you wouldn't've see mine
or anybody else's parents calling up to get the pool
slabbed over in my memory. But one kid—*one kid*—
chokes on a mouthful of mallow and the mollycoddlers
get a beloved tradition banned for life, one where
the risk was part of the excitement in the first place.
Listen to these rules pretending you've never heard
them before: Each player puts a big marshmallow in
his mouth, does not swallow, says "chubby bunny,"
adds another big marshmallow, says "chucky bucky,"
adds another, tries not to choke, says "chuh-ee uh-ee,"
and stuffs in another one or five or thirteen until one
player is left standing. Remind you of any other games
with the word Chicken in the title? Players worried
about asphyxiation turn back early, spit their goo into
a bucket, and hit the water fountain. Those who want
to win proceed. Without the risk, Chuh-ee Uh-ee would
be nothing at all: kid stuff.

Thursday

SANDRA EXEGETES

This is the first year, girls, I've had to explain to my cabin that "be real" does not mean sulk around in your sighberry eyeliner. We're all tired. We're supposed to be tired. After a half-hour of in-bunk flashlight tag, sticking a couple of hands in a warm water bowl, and a spooky forbidden round of Light as a Feather, Stiff as a Board, we're looking at a low 5.5 hours per night. Good luck finding a way around it. A woman's greatest knack is how well she can hide how much sleep she's been missing. There's a little tally board inside each of us labeled, "Number of days since someone has told me I look tired" that resets itself whenever we make the mistake of looking like we feel. And the alternative? Even if you fulfill obligations, party like you mean it, and somehow get your sleep, your decisions will be too well-informed to be spontaneous. You'll never be susceptible to life. And that goes double for this week, divas. We don't need your gears shifting at full speed, we need you able to hold your foot behind your head.

COMPLAINT

Every time I love someone, you set them free.

ALL THE ARMIES OF MY BOOT

Nobody blames you, demon. You show a deep passion. You work long hours. But you must've had an inkling: How many pentagrams did you think we'd allow on one girl's bedpost? On how many summer days did you think gloves would hide your sloppy stigmatas before a staff member figured out something was up? Hey now. Let's not make this into a thing. Tears aren't evil. Show your grit with a stoic exit. You can give Susie a last shiver if you want, take a last look through her tiny windows, whisper a final corrosive in her ear. She will miss you at times. Back-talking will sting when she sees whom she's hurting. Whipped cream on steak will lose appeal. Flirting with rebels will still an entirely different set of voices. I was thinking I'd let you cast yourself out—there's dignity in that—but get yourself gone by the end of the workday. I'd let you finish out the week but we need her bubbly for tomorrow's relay. Hold up your head when you get back home—the other demons are in your same sad boat. They wouldn't be in Hell if they hadn't done something wrong. Nobody there wasn't caught failing.

*

Dear Mom,

It's dawning on me, the disadvantage I'm at not having
been raised in a bilingual household.

    Billy

TWO DAYS, FOURTEEN HOURS

All it takes is a glance out the craft hut window to imagine the real party that must be happening up in the cold, I'm talking *cold*, mesosphere right now, daily burning through meteors like 30-packs of Keystone, and to picture how unconvincing our in-the-moment expressions must seem from up there. But down here, the alternative is dim and bratty and nothing I want to look at. Had this one kid who kept trying to hide up in his bunk before activities, lying real still like I wouldn't notice, offering bribes when I collected him by force and sat him beside me. Then a switch flipped. He had this great night at skits, laughing louder than anybody, and became self-sufficient for half a day. Now every time I see him, he makes this bittersweet face and tells me how many days and hours of camp are left cause he doesn't want to go home. I can empathize, the way trying to live in the moment is like trying to find the button that turns off the reverb on the karaoke machine. I had a couple of his cabinmates heave that kid in the pool with his clothes on, but there's only so much one counselor can do to drown out a kid's brain's wants.

PASS ME THAT FLASHLIGHT

A woman was killed in a wreck at the tunnel five years ago tonight. She died in the snow from the fire, drowned, her spirit condemned to wander the waterways, weeping and searching for her children until the end of time. After what seemed like hours, she heard a far off bugle blast, and then silence. Her baby was still alive. Was he looking for his head? She went home and collapsed into bed, wondering what happened to the man on the motorcycle. The next morning, she went to the bathroom, and there, scrawled on the mirror in blood: *I am the viper. I'm on the fifth floor.* She realized then that the old man at the gas station had been trying to warn her. To this day, the light of her torch still can be seen on stormy nights. To this day, the fathers of the village wear scars as a reminder. To this day, La Malhora appears at the crossroads whenever someone is going to die. That baby was my daughter. That psycho was me.

FRIDAY

*

Dear Mom,

Let us not fear death. There is too much to do while yet on this earth.

Billy

GROGG CORNERS A CAMPER

Peek here, progeny. You got slacks to tell me I can't strafe into my own square yardage with a rage-gage sport-slick auto-rotation twelve-forty and pluck me up something for the spit? I respect you're unalert to the factuals. Fair as fare, sure—you're up in your tusk spire, not knowing how my days roll out, thinking up muck to hock. It get cold up there, Senator? There's an honor in my twelve you don't cohere. A subset of somesuch would be *lucky* to go out with permanence by means of my craft. If I'm a monkey—and there's exhibits to the situals—then at some point the critters of this greenscape globe ought to learn themselves some avoidance procession. What we cannot abide is weakness by and by. Critters. Heh, heh. "Ooh, look at me. So mystic in my fur. Think I'll prostate myself in this smoothie-black road and see what shakes." Well what you won't do is pass on no dumbslick spunk, Thumper. And so the cyclone ongoes.

CAMPFIRES: AN UNPROMPTED HISTORY

These days we'll do a "Pirate's Cove" theme one year, "Adventure Inland" the next, then something controversial like "A Week at the Movies" before returning to "Pirate's Cove," but there was a time when Indians were the theme, the pull, the selling point of every camp in the nation. Boys slept in teepees and arrowed straw buffalos. Each camp had a brave to call its own, right there on the front of the pamphlet. Solemn full-headdress Indian was more fun, plainclothes nature survivalist Indian had more dignity. Later, due to the rightful concerns of the Moms, natives were replaced by safe whites in redface who'd hung around the real thing for a long weekend, taking notes. My own Pap used to polish his face up burnt orange then monotone to the kids about the tribal councils, the first Thanksgiving, headdress color combos, names that're almost sentences, swinging from trees to cover tracks when pursued, and of nightly meetings at the burning council ring. Some bits were of disputed authenticity, like the ole hand over mouth "wa-wa-wa," but it was loud and felt great to do. Great enough that everybody felt their racism shedding, letting themselves think of Indians as this far off dodo dream. But then the soldiers killed Hitler, came on home, squinted at how their boys got funny, and we soon cut the teepees and resident redman from the prop roster. We scrubbed the campfires white and used them for their hypnotic potential, for singing Eagles hits, for life-changing emotional appeals, for tales of hook-handed lady-scrapers. They were too pretty to discontinue, too much fun, and budding girls looked too good in their light.

ICE-BREAKER

So I say the situation then you each say what you'd do. You're flummoxed in a locked zoo at night, in boots and a knit cap but otherwise bare, there's been a drought, you and she have just this evening had a tough talk after which it's clear that you're the one who loves her more. Sleep eludes you, it's a leap year, the baby test came back "baby," the zoo's owner is a registered sex offender and he's told you more about it than law demands, money is thankfully not an issue, the cages have all been opened, the electric fences have been down since the storm, you had a reasonably happy childhood, and you're allowed to pick two of the following: a flashlight, a mirror, self-assurance, compassion, a full moon, a phone call, a decoy, a harpoon, passable French, a walkman, batteries, a map, and a clue. The first part of my question isn't a question: I'm so sorry to have put you in this position. The second part of my question, on the condition that you are man enough to let her go: I will love the child as if it were my own.

QUESTION

I feel like we're missing some campers. Are we missing some campers?

MY FACE HURTS

It's so hard to command emotions, Fun Camp! It just is. But we believe, don't we, that commanding the good ones, like, "I'm having a smiling time in the managed danger of this hot field," is a shot at actually feeling happy and that commanding the bad ones, like, "I'm hungry," or "Trees suck," or "Fire in the building!" is a shot at nothing at all? Unless it's Oscar season? Put another way: Is fake it 'til you make it just for job interviews, or for when flossing too? Or still another: Which would win the genuine face pageant: The "everything is good and ends badly" face? The "not getting as much sleep as I'd prefer" face that's so popular around here? Or is it the one that implies, as the young pop star once declared at the receipt of her own Commander of Bad Feelings award, that *this world is bullshit*? God, I hope not. How embarrassing for the friendly and what a coup for the sultry. My closest approximation of sultry is pouty, and I never think I'm being pouty when I'm being pouty. How Holly reminds me I'm being pouty is by telling me it's important to try and enjoy this. This being anything, whatever's in front of us.

PATTERN I NOTICED

At a belief club meeting, a newcomer asks a question
so elemental that the members laugh, delighted, having
forgotten it could be asked. The newcomer squirms and
the members are quick to apologize. They applaud her
marksmanship, her rigor. Then they secure a time for
the next week's meeting. They're not trying to dodge
the question. They think they've answered it.

QUICK ANNOUNCEMENT
BEFORE LUNCH

A word to the cultists—yes, you in your robes, the boys who cried apocalypse: We're pulling the plug. It's a little solipsistic to have witnessed a few distant mushroom-like smoke clouds and assume a wrecked world, parents all dead, and that God has chosen the innocents of Fun Camp for a new Eden. All you tittering fence-sitters: Think it's an accident this new one true faith came from Boys Cabin 1? Continuation of the species is man's oldest pickup line. I'm sure the gophers you blood-sacrificed would be real happy to learn their deaths are wrapped up in the wet dreams of some teenage would-be Christs. Speaking of, Jason, you're paying for that tablecloth you're wearing, and Tad, whose 501s did you massacre to make that Jesus sash? You look like runner-up in a West Virginia beauty pageant. Who's booing? Hey—who was just booing? Any more of you want to make a midnight raid on the iPhone closet, you'll find I've moved the phones to an undisclosed site and the batteries to the vault under the snack shack. Nature-knowing is about avoidance and you're all too wrecked to get there alone. You've got fifty-one weeks out of the year to check your scores and count your dead. Surrender this one to fun.

BEAN PEOPLE

Today we make bean people. We'll each glue six to ten beans to a sheet of construction paper—light-colored is best, blue or gray or yellow, so the beans look like they're three-dimensional, which they are. Then we're going to paint faces on the beans, different expressions but especially smiling, and draw legs and arms on the paper around the beans. Hands and feet too if you like. Shirts and ties and jobs and bills, fill out the lives of your bean people with the richness of your imaginations. You can make them into fish, cats, dogs, birds, bugs, whatever. You can make them skate, ski, crawl, fly, any G-rated thing at all, just by drawing what their limbs are doing. But before we begin, let's pass the big sack of beans around, careful not to spill, and each take a turn reaching a hand in deep. Aren't the beans cool and smooth? They almost feel wet, don't they? This is one of those shortcuts to pleasure, kids, sticking your hand deep in some beans. We don't ask why it's so good, we just be thankful.

COMPLAINT

Getting stuck nodding while Chef Grogg holds forth makes my mouth feel all, what, like full of rocks and slobbering. Could he not talk to us as a rule?

ROY

I've got no peroxide for that hurt. If he doesn't love you back, girlfriend: a story.

Roy, a baby, was named for a real man, cowboy Rogers. But all Roy did was bathe horses in a swimming pool. He stared out on the delta and beyond, to his sad soul.

A director one day passed him. "You have become a man now!" the director whispered in surprise.

"But I have no money," Roy said.

That day, in an agent's office: "I have your man."

"Nobody wants a cowboy star," the agent mentioned.

Roy got on the horse. "Something in mind?" He had the look all right.

At his film, a non-white man gave him his first crack of cocaine and Roy was never the same. In his mind, he bathed horses of the rainbow. His Mom forgave him for forgetting her address, watching his reruns and happily singing his song out and proud. Roy's dad said sorry for leaving.

Roy got dry. Roy went to schools and told his Tale of Caution. Always, when he told them, children laughed but obeyed his commands.

SUMMER LOVIN'
TORTURE PARTY

When the gaslight blinks to say my inspiration tank's low, I look to the Middle Ages. A man back then who had a beef with his neighbor didn't hire a suit, he simply challenged the neighbor to a battle to the death. Since God wouldn't let an innocent man down, whoever remained standing was righteous. The other favored mode until Trial by Jury yawned its way into common practice in the 13th century was the Ordeal, in which the accused would have to walk through fire, carry a hot iron, or run the gauntlet. And if you passed, you were innocent—opposite logic of the Puritan "If she burns, she's a witch" model. Pretty sensible, if grisly. For me, nothing puts my life on a path like a good coin flip or a straw draw. Give the divine room to do its mysterious thing. I feel for the courts, making their judgments, but their errors are well-documented. When an innocent man finds himself strapped to a chair he'll never stand up from, it's the outcome of a fallen world without the courage to leave a thing like justice up to chance.

*

Dear Mom,

What have you done?

Billy

LOGISTICALLY, A REAL MOMENTUM-WRECKER

One night at skits back when I was a camper, one of the tight-jeaned older heartthrob guys from Cabin 1 got up and said, "Here's a song I like," and they'd rigged up the PA to play a seven-minute David Bazan song, the first I'd heard by him. I later acquired the guy's whole catalogue, listened my way through Bazan's ascent / descent from sleepy Christian sweetie pie to conflicted Christian questioner to pissed-off agnostic antagonizer. All his best music is from that middle period when he was in the thick of it. The track in question, "Secret of the Easy Yoke," is a gorgeous downer about wanting to know God while ever put off by His parishioners. "I still have never seen you," Bazan sings in the chorus, "and some days I don't love you at all." After the bridge, there's an instrumental verse that functions as an outro. When the song finished playing that night at skits, the heartthrob got back up and told of the time he saw Bazan play the song live. Bazan allegedly played it just as he had on the album until the third (no longer instrumental) verse, in which he sang, "In a moment, I'm alive again." So after the show, heartthrob asked Bazan why he didn't sing the line on the album version. Bazan said, "Because that's the verse where

I reconcile with God. But you have to figure that part out for yourself." And I thought, *This guy talked to a musician after a concert? Badass.* And then Brent bought all the albums and then I bought all the albums. And on YouTube there's a more recent video of Bazan playing the song live and he just ends it at the bridge.

QUESTION

When a devout man swears with the explicit intent of
remaining relevant to the culture at large, isn't he just
not-swearing in disguise?

WARM FUZZY

Boy w/ Frosty Tips in Line at Dinner – w4m – 13: You, a lake pirate from the wrong side of the tracks. Me, an unconventionally pretty self-starter often beside a huskier "wingwoman" type. You asked if I knew whether we could start with two cornbreads. I didn't know and said so. You said not to worry about it, practically feeling me up with eye contact. You had a sweatshirt tucked into a pair of black shorts so baggy they could fit two people—an invitation? Later I found out we have to start with one cornbread and wait for everybody to go through the line before going back for more. Write me back what color hoodie I was wearing. Or if you already know who this is, come find me at quiet time tomorrow. Bring chapstick.

ALL THESE HURTS

Dried burnt macaroni cheese on a pot that big means it's time to break out the steel wool, Puddy. Keep swishing it like that in circles. Now pour that orangey water out and see how you're doing. Long way to go. I worry over sanitation exactly as much as I worry over the Large Hedron Collider whose future self stopped it from making a Big Bang, and over a God who kicked idolatry down the list of don'ts to make room for Higgs' particles, and over the seasonal question, "Is my love life just an experiment testing the potential correlation between hairnets and invisibility? On how low a girl's got to wear her top to get a little attention in this getup?" All these hurts on all these timelines add up to a *Twilight Zone* where everybody knows the forthcoming twist and discusses it openly but will gasp with true feeling when it comes. I believe this, and when I really think about it, I cover my neck with my hands. But then the other ninety percent of the time, I revert to the adage that goes, "Has anyone known true loss but those who've opened an avocado to find it's a couple days past ripe?" I wish I was rich enough to look on the back of meats for traces of chronic discomfort. I wish I'd live long enough to see how far past our own globe we can get. I wish I got to laugh at the sun with mean, real confidence for not noticing how long we've been growing apart, for not having enough mass to explode as a supernova. How much? How much do I worry about *what*? Oh. Infrequently but desperately. What if a kid got struck down from mystery microbes in our chili-mac, Puddy? You'd kill yourself. We all would.

MORALS OF THIS EVENING'S SKITS, AS FAR AS DAVE CAN MAKE OUT, FROM LEAST TROUBLING TO MOST

All school shootings would have been prevented had the shooters gone to Fun Camp.

Refusing to participate in pranks means you're majorly asking to get pranked.

A beer sip and you're blitzed.

Everyone deserves everything that happens.

Chef Grogg is incomprehensible and a little creepy yet may possess a heart of gold.

Grogg's chicken potpies cause widespread diarrhea.

Girls Cabin 2 will make out with anybody.

That submarine skit can sustain 20 years of viewing.

A compilation of Tad Gunnick quotes read aloud from a ripped spiral sheet both qualifies as a skit and warrants a standing O.

Dave and Holly tolerate being mocked.

FLIGHT OF THE BORING

Illegal elopement from the campsite constitutes the unfun child's most drastic method of resisting our intensive treatment structure. Often times, the flight constitutes a last-ditch attempt at hanging on to what our little renegade deems his best self. As if he's in an objective position to appraise his own personality! Four out of five times you'll find him hiding out in that old bunker the kids think we don't know about. You yell at him, freak him out, tell him about the Malhara that stalks these woods, or the Jackal looking to make a ritual sacrifice, or the peeved natives looking to re-gift disease blankets to the chilled ancestors of crafty pioneers—just wing it, really, get him crying. Drive slow on the way home so he calms down, then switch to Good Cop. Here's where the camper will complain that the leaders of Fun Camp "just don't get my sense of humor," or he'll fumble around with the idea that fun is neither an absolute nor a choice. The child's views should be applauded for their well-intendedness, then refuted. A counselor's greatest joy is when, in a Come to Fun Camp moment such as this, the boring child expresses true contrition, and repeats with you the three tenets of surrender: I suck but I know it. I'm bland but I'm working on it. I am hated by those who will someday revere me, for as their self-awareness slackens, my power grows.

SATURDAY

LADS OF THEIR NUMBER

Who here can tell me how many bears came out of the woods and mauled the forty-two youths who called Elisha a baldhead? Who can tell me what God did to Uzzah when he steadied an ark he had no business steadying? Here's a hint: The answer isn't, "Normally, I could look it up." Who can tell me what slithery creatures venomed the Israelites to death when they got to whining about their rustic living conditions? Anybody? This is bad news, children. I should've known the anti-memorization generation isn't gonna make an exception for sanctified texts. You got the Word called up on your Ken-Doll right beside *Vampire Angst Academy*, ready to go, like your pocket is your brain. It's not your fault, you poor damaged darlings, you one nation underdogs, you bushel-covered lights of mine. Your bankrupt public schools won't even let you heed commandments in nice round numbers, rail on Darwin in a written-portion-of-the-Chem-test pinch, pray through first period in sleepy reverence, or perform any of the tricks that allowed me to clock in at school without absorbing their slop. If you haven't heard it from anyone, you're hearing it from me: You are what you memorize. Should we stand? Should we sing? You'd like that, but no. Instead, repeat after me:

Then two bears came out of the woods and mauled forty-two of the youths. Then two bears came out of the woods and mauled forty-two of the youths. Then two bears came out of the woods and mauled forty-two of the youths. Stop laughing.

LISTEN TO ME

Because you are children and I am a man, and thus I've had more opportunities to notice patterns than you have.

Because even as I stuff myself stupid at lunch, a controlling interest in me understands I'll be starving by dinner.

Because everything that makes *me* irrational has been tidily wrapped up in sex.

Because a lady I knew would've signed on to pair up with me for the long haul if I'd asked her.

Because my biggest gripes are with soft men I'll never meet.

Because I own my own house.

Because I've cajoled barroom stories from mirthy Jacks who'll up and leave a bar at the sound of the German language.

Because I could tell you about Kansas and Kant, Ken Starr and cover letters.

Because I know tricks for keeping myself from crying.

Because I'd kick each of your asses at *The Price is Right*.

Because I memorized the verbal fallacies and blow this whistle whenever I hear one.

Because I've raised brows by wit alone.

Because I can tell you why certain movies are good with words you'd use wrong.

Because I registered your sense of wonder and factored it into the way I regard you.

Because I could trick even the savviest among you, and have already. And will.

Because the sting of failure has humbled me without my say so.

Because I annually get worse at lying to myself and better at avoiding bare truths.

Because the worry my birthday causes me points to a big fact I'm beginning to allow myself to acknowledge.

Because I'd do alright in the wild for a time.

Because I could kill each of you with both arms bound.

Because I know just when to kill a joke.

I KNOW WE'RE TRAMPLING HISTORY BUT

If you think back far enough, what *wasn't* built on an Indian burial ground? Was I the ghost of a native, I bet I'd be pretty understanding about where my conquerors build their resorts. The sacred's got a clock like anything. Me, I'd like my grave marked and mowed for a solid century, long enough for everyone who could've ever loved me to join me. After that, they're free to erect a fresh Dillard's on my once-marked bones. I owe a shot at discounts to the not yet dead.

GROGG CORNERS A CAMPER

Feel this knot. Yes, touch it. Post-veto, I was told my back would've been practed and kneeded had I narrated that my paindaggers had come on sudden in the a.m. Gander at a man's leased camp shack, then ask me how long I'll keep up the ole wince-and-grit for. Death, to thems, is the pickle you ask for none of, please. You might still get served a briny cuke in and on and beside your tray—it may yes happen—but some pimply shluck is gonna get the shitcan for it. That there is some blood-weary optimism in my spectation. Surprised for me, colt? This is worth leaping a parisian fence for, kiddo, unless your constituency cuts his own checks. A prior history is a costly flopping redundancy. My nightly prayers, in order of downward likeness: one is for said-mentioned outfromers to pod me in for a medicinal autotuning, two is for a blonde-bosomed young Montrealite staffer to arrive one summer, burned and beautiful, who'll hitch me to her wagon and socialize me. Scram in case of either.

WE LOVE FUN CAMP, YES WE DO

Damned if those kids don't take some of the cock out of my walk, though. Delightful isolated moments, you bet, but after morning counselor meetings I get that pit-level dread, mouthing soundless expletives. Dread where the heart beats faster and the body deflates. Dread where they can smell that you don't want to say hey or lead line-up cheers louder than the other cabins. They pick up on more than you think, yet they never pick up on that particular thing you're so sure they know. Once-over a she-counselor and you feel a guilt the Catholics keep trying to claim for themselves, a guilt that goes, "If my kids only knew this heart, hoo-boy." And if they did? They're all spies ready to sell you out for an attaboy, new zeal smoothing their faces to bland mush. By the end of the week, I can't tell my own boys apart. I cover it, addressing each of them with a "Cabin 3, *what*," which they've come to respond to more than their own names anyway.

Saturday

THE MAGIC OF SUMMER

I want us all to do an experiment together. Ready? [Pause ten seconds.] In the last ten seconds, each of you has forgotten just a tiny fraction of the math skills you picked up in school last year. Isn't that wonderful? They can learn you up with whatever they want mid-August through early June, but in the interim, if you choose not to use it? [Clap hands free of unwanted math.] Gone for months. And that's adulthood, kids: an endless string of summers full of sweet choice. It's as fun as it sounds, and it's never terrifying, not if you're smart about it.

HELLO CLONE, I WILL SAY

Myself having a religious background can understand your point. Sometimes I too wonder if identical twins have souls or only half-souls. Until cloning has been fully researched, no one knows if clones will live productive lives as human beings. As humans, however, we have placed ourselves on top of a ladder, God's power in our hands, and with time and research, any bumps and risks can be smoothed just like anything in the middle of being discovered. After school some days, I picture me in a clone sisterhood where we gang up on the prime-numbered sisters, good-naturedly, though I am not a prime number in the scenario. Seeing versions of ourselves everywhere is cautionary, and we exercise like madwomen then strip down to our underwear in full-length mirrors to compare. We all kiss different clones of the same boy and mix ourselves up, sometimes on purpose, in case it tastes somehow different. We get old and pass kidneys around and get mad at Dad together. All our birthdays fall on the same day and that day is my birthday.

Saturday

COMPLAINT

This is going to give me away but, whatever. Can you, Holly, an adult, presumably knowledgeable in the world's rubbytouchy ways, tell me in good conscience that it's *my* mind caught in the gutter when I lose my composure while singing, "Cool and creamy / We like cool and creamy / Cool and creamy / We like it a lot. / / *Do you like it in your face?* / Yes I like it in my face. / *In your face?* / In my face! / In our face!" One go-through I could handle, but three? When in the second verse, we sing, "Do you like it in your ears?" And in the third, "hair?" Can you honesty tell me the song was not written with the intent of making naïve children sing about ejaculate? That an earlier draft was not instead called "Hot and Creamy" but that the author's buddy got the bong out of his mouth long enough to suggest the author cover his tracks just a little? The truth is: You pulled me from morning cheers because *I get the joke*. The truth is: You barely got through your own scold with a straight face.

*

Dear Mom,

How often have you asked me what I would do without
you? Five days apart, and we seem to have our answer:
I would live, Mother. I live.

Billy Matthews

HARD YEAR FOR EVERYBODY

This game is Counselors-Only and begins on brooms. Fanciful, the way we like it, based on a movie my friend made when he saw a book a pretty girl was reading in the contemporary cinematic facelift of *The Crucible*. You drink and ride and drink and span the blacktop until you fall over. We rush around you and say what you'll be, based on how you're lying. Like one girl was spread-eagle so she became a patriotic ornithologist. One girl was dead so she became a ticket dispenser on I-90. One girl never fell so we cursed her children's blood. It's just fun, Holly. If you've got a better way of discovering God's plan for my postgraduate life, scrawl it on a donut receipt, find some bored talons to stick it in, then tape up the bird and mail it wherever my soft body crumbled.

COMPLAINT

What's so fun about Water Pong? Since when is hydration a penalty?

CANTEEN BUCK CAPER

It's come to the staff's attention that a traitor among you has started her own canteen buck mint. This camper would need access to a Xerox machine, the yesteryear restraint to keep from spending her last canteen buck, pale green cardstock paper, the moral bankruptcy not to care, and the brains to pull it off, so already that rules out most of you, including all first-timers and all inner city scholarship kids. A part of me just wants to shut down camp early over this mint—I am serious as a broken pact here—a mint whose counterfeit product is realistic enough to fool even myself, having surveyed thousands of spent bucks in search of the mark of the fake. It's the fact that I can use the word *thousands* that tipped us off, our week-end sales usually hitting the mid to high hundreds. That and the tummy troubles evident among a certain contingent of Cabin 2 girls. And the series of increasingly elaborate disguises said girls donned to purchase well past their camper daily health limit, a disguising that was permitted at the time for its ingenuity, for the "This is what camp is all about" feeling it gave on-duty staffers. And a Twix supply that ran out on day two, Twix being the fluke corporate item our townie vendor vends us, meaning our supplies are down to such complaint card name-checked perennials as Miss Marie's Chewbarb Taffy and Mishima Confectionary's Mangoflave Gingercakes, and so there will be no cause for fold-up chair-kicking outbursts when I pronounce the canteen closed until the culprits come forward and Stop. Ruining. Everything. Did I mention that each cabin is currently being searched, starting with Girls Cabin 2? Confess in the next thirty seconds and there's a fresh hot cola in it for you, brewed personally by Ole Maud, a sweet blind townie whose story'll just break your heart if you let her tell it.

TESTIMONY

Last year, I didn't do like I said. I said I was going to change and for awhile I did change but then I went back. I went back to what I was before I changed without even realizing I'd gone back. Sometimes I would remember I had changed and would try to change back to how I had changed and then I would change again. But my friends would not see the change, or else they would see the change but they wouldn't like the change because we had made friends before the change, and they would try to change me back. So I would change back. Now being back here has reminded me that I really do want to change, and what I want this time is to change for good. And I want you all to hold me accountable and in exchange I will hold you accountable. I feel really bad that I didn't change before. Really, really bad. Thank you.

SNOW DAY

In half a year, the Caucasians among you will be more so. On the front end of winter, we'll spend Christmas nursing our generosity, New Years kissing it goodbye. On the back end, we coast through Ash Wednesday fine if we notice it at all, spend Easter wearing the colors we've painted our eggs. It's between the first snow and the last time Dad runs his salty white car through the wash that you won't believe there was ever a summer, ever an us here together now. As the arc of your relationship to snow begins to mirror that of the romances the facially symmetrical among you are cooking up now, you'll have to try to float on those perennial comforts: Friends who wait outside your house so they can shock you with something wet, stinging shops whose temperature regulators overcompensate for what the outside is up to, satellite electronics, parents at jobs, oversleeping, sugar drinks, the taste of fruits whose vacillating prices you won't notice until the day it's you doing the buying. I say this not to ease the shock of winter but to ease the shock over the shock. The sooner you realize winter is annual, the sooner you'll buckle down on those grades and start dreaming of a college in the never-fading sun of some golden country.

Saturday

WARM FUZZY

I hate you, Tad. You don't just introduce yourself to a girl on the dock and chat her up about the little podunks you're both from, discover how much you've got in common, sit real close, get the crazy idea you and her ought to run off the dock in all your clothes, jump hand in hand in the lake, together invent new swimstokes, laugh lots, thank the girl for the swim, and then go ask some slut like Helena Johnson on the Midnight Hike. As if you didn't feel that once-in-a-campweek connection with the girl on the dock! As if you had a realer talk with Helena Johnson! Did you know that until last month she had a boyfriend three years older than her and that they did about everything you can do together that isn't technically sex? She told me the first night here. So it's not just that you're picking her over me, it's that you're willing to risk contracting some sexually nasty infections by just kissing her. And yet what kills me is I know you won't. You're untouchable. You're Tad Gunnick. As I write this, you and a semicircle of hangers-on are headed for the pool with Bee Gees on repeat in all your heads, so sure you're God's gift to strutting. And she's Helena Johnson, spilling out of cups two letters down the alphabet from mine. And then there's me, scrawling notes in a hot craft hut, sure to be rewarded for my abstinence with opportunities for more abstinence. Watch as it starts to look less like a choice.

*

Dear Mom,

Forget me. When the time comes, I will send for Johannes.

Billy Matthews, Cabin 3

PEAKED AT FOURTEEN

We hit dinner in a daze, you and I, after a lively session of getting told what. Some girls cried, and we almost did too. We'd chased and caught the ecstatic moment, mistook it for a house to live in. It felt like shivers and coffee and God's favor. The meal tasted good, pork chops and peas with rolls and red punch. And when you were made to sing a song for having elbows up on the table, you laughed and you sang—something mockable, Journey or Styx. On the verge of some big thing, we asked Dave himself if we could skip campfire so we could work out the terms of our new selves, and he said that he respected that but still felt campfire was where we needed to be. We understood and poured gravy on Doreen, who was a sport and later got us back big. At the fire, we knew Dave had been right and sang "Peaceful, Easy Feeling" and "Brown Eyed Girl" and my only earnest "Kumbaya" to date. After most had scattered, we huddled and squirted water to sizzle on the embers, too beat to talk. That was my best night, my best self, and that was three whole camps ago. What have we been doing wrong, Amber? What broke in us?

FROM A FIELD ON A MOUNTAIN

Look, everybody: We rolled out the stars for you tonight. We softened the grass. We briskened the air just enough that you'd need each other. I want so much for you as a gaggle of campers, but as individuals I can barely keep your faces in focus. As I look out on the field of you now, huddling up in your sleeping bags, I see selves feeding selves feeding selves. I see, "What do these people think of me?" and "Am I unique?" and "Am I funny?" and "Am I worthy of love?" And to all those questions, I offer a hearty resounding shrug, and I implore you, when you go home tomorrow, to watch an entire serious dramatic film on fast forward. I'm trying to do for delusion what Clark Gable did for the undershirt. There's a confidence chemical that suddenly gets produced like crazy in puberty that explains why five-sixths of you think you know so much. Even now, as you scoff out into the night, that's the chemical at work, and knowing about the chemical makes it no less potent. The goal is to harness that chemical and to run with it as far as you can so that when doubt catches up, you'll be surrounded by people who angle their bodies toward you and nod brightly when you speak. I've got more to say—I've always got more to say—but for now

I'm out of lozenges. Be sure and wave at me tomorrow morning before you go. I'll keep walking, but I will see you.

SUNDAY MORNING

THAT'S IT?

Yeah, Sunday pulls the rug out from everyone. When we wake, there's always some group from far-off already gone, goodbyes unsaid. We treat Sunday like a full day in our heads all week, but then it comes and it's just a morning—a morning spent packing. All these suddenly-concerned boys run around looking for plastic bags to keep the moldy wet clothes that've been balled under the bed all week from infecting their less-moldy dry clothes. We approach each other, newly sheepish, holding copies of the group photo and sharpies, saying, "Are you going to the Fun Retreat weekend in October? I think I'm going, are you going?" We mop and squint and sing a last song. Then parents start showing up, smiling like they belong. Like they have a clue what went on here. Like they've ever felt a thing in their lives.

*

Dear Mom,

For much of the week, I'd forgotten how slow regular mail is. By the time you get this, I'll have already been home for three days or so. Please disregard the last few letters. They were hasty. If my room is still available, I'd like to stay. I do ask, however, that you take a look at your schedule so we may set aside an evening when I'll outline the changes I'd like to see our family implement in the coming quarter, such as you learning to make cornbread and us eating on the porch when it's nice out and us getting a pool and playing kickball and having food fights and you letting me pick on Deirdre when it's in a funny way. I look forward to returning to my room, my toys, a bathroom with a lock, and of course, Johannes. I hope you have shown him my pictures as I asked.

With affection,
William

BEST FRIENDS SHOULD
BE TOGETHER

We'll get a pair of those half-heart necklaces so every ask n' point reminds us we are one glued duo. We'll send real letters like our grandparents did, handwritten in smart cursive curls. We'll extend cell plans and chat through favorite shows like a commentary track just for each other. We'll get our braces off on the same day, chew whole packs of gum. We'll nab some serious studs but tell each other everything. Double-date at a roadside diner exactly halfway between our homes. Cry on shoulders when our boys fail us. We'll room together at State, cover the walls floor-to-ceiling with incense posters of pop dweebs gone wry. See how beer feels. Be those funny cute girls everybody's got an eye on. We'll have a secret code for hot boys in passing. A secret dog named Freshman Fifteen we'll have to hide in the rafters during inspection. Follow some jam band one summer, grooving on lawns, refusing drugs usually. Get tattoos that only spell something when we stand together. I'll be maid of honor in your wedding and you'll be co-maid with my sister but only cause she'd disown me if I didn't let her. We'll start a store selling just what we like. We'll name our firstborn daughters after one another, and if our husbands don't like it, tough. Lifespans being what they are, we'll be there for each other when our men have passed, and all the friends who come to visit our assisted living condo will be dazzled by what fun we still have together. We'll be the kind of besties who make outsiders wonder if they've ever known true friendship, but we won't even notice how sad it makes them and they won't bring it up because you and I will be so caught up in the fun, us marveling at how not-good it never was.

THE SUDDEN IMPOSITION OF CHORES

We make the hulks Dismantle the Stage and Stack Benches. To the Least Improved goes Bathroom Duty. The older kids know to call Trash Pickup, which is job code for Make Out in the Woods. For Girls Cabin 1, we put together an algorithm and found that when you factor in the bitching, the required supervision, and how cranky they are from staying up all night comparing the Very Real Talks they'd each had with Tad Gunnick, it actually saves time to exempt them from chores. Really, though, no matter what jobs you give these kids, you're gonna catch some flack: "Aren't there people whose *job* it is to mop and shine and sweep and scour?" and "Didn't we pay *big bucks* to come here?" and "Are we not remarkable precocious youths to be *catered* to?" and "Do we not *deserve*?" All valid points. Cleaning just isn't on-message. If I had my way, we'd forget all about the security deposit we so sorely need returned and instead would wake the campers the last morning by balloon-pelting them in their unsuspecting bunks, chasing them out of their cabins and onto the rec field where their own arsenal waits, and we'd engage them in an epic campers vs. counselors water balloon bout, have them greet their moms sopping—give those moms a sense of where their money went.

QUESTION

Dave and Holly, how old are you? And is camp like your whole job all year or is there other stuff?

THE MISSING LINES

I was checking the clothesline for warm fuzzies when I noticed Tad Gunnick climbing up on the bench Dave stands on to make announcements, and there a small crowd of us gathered around him.

"What do you call a cheese that isn't yours?" Tad asked us. We began to respond, but he continued. "Why did the chicken cross the road? Where do bats get their energy? Knock, knock, who's there, the interrupting cow. How do you know when a blonde has been making chocolate chip cookies? How many hucksters does it take to screw in a light bulb? Two guys are getting drunk at the top of a very tall building and one says to the other, 'I bet you I can jump out the window, fly around, and come back safe.' Yo mama's so fat. You might be a redneck if. What's Lorena Bobbitt's favorite kind of soda? What do you call a dog that can tell time?"

After awhile, some campers among us began to grumble. *Who is this Tad Gunnick*, we wondered, *who offers jokes and withholds the punchlines?* Tad guessed at our concern and said, "The time will soon come when I am no longer here and you will have to provide your own punchlines."

"But why, Tad?" one said.

"Where will you go?" said another.

Tad answered, "Arizona State," and slipped away from us in the confusion.

DOWN THE MOUNTAIN

Kids come to me in their little tears, wanting to know one thing: "How do I take Fun Camp down the mountain, Chaplain Bernadette?" You come here and have this literally mountaintop experience then go home again to your old friends, your old neighbors, your old parents, them ready to snatch you back into old boring habits. Well don't you let them! You can water balloon bombard from any tower in this nation. You can whittle Mom a totem in your room any winter Sunday. On inner city sidewalks you can nature hike through the machete-blazed footpaths of your own minds. You can joke like Tad. You can skit on the street. Be Fun Camp to your commute-weary parents, Fun Camp to your grave mustachioed principal, Fun Camp to the salt-of-the-earth cigarette flickers loitering up and down the promenade. All of them saying, "Sweep this mess! Read this book! Do this math problem!" Kids, what pleasure has an exciting person ever gleaned proofing an obtuse? The proof'll be all around you! If you keep your heart locked up in a camp that knows best, no authority's got a chance. Now turn in your songbooks to page 12, "We Are the Champions," and really focus on the words, really knowing in the heart of your heart that we win. As we stand. And as we sing.

ONE WEEK

One week? So many sticky memories in such a disposable duration seems impossible. In seventy-five years, you'll be grizzled on some hospital bed, leaning too hard on memories to divert you from a slow death, struggling to recall your husband's name, hard-pressed to find a memory about which you can confidently say, "That was in my thirties," but speaking in complete paragraphs about the boy you met when he came plowing into you at kickball, about when you yelled "gin!" during Spades and made him laugh, about the conspiratorial lunch table whispers you and his friends shared over whether he'd be your boyfriend, about the stiff goodbye when he left a night early to get to an aunt's wedding, about the cheek peck he gave you, and about the note to him you'd folded into your sock. A note that scratched your ankle with each step as you went to meet him and again on the way back. His mom was watching from the car, smiling weird. You were from the city and camp was your first time seeing a real night sky. "I never told you all this, Dad," old you will say to your old husband. "I kept it a secret." But you've told him for years. He eggs you on cause he sees how you love to tell it, how each time you think of it, it's a revelation, a gift you got you.

Gabe Durham's writings have appeared in *Hobart, Mid-American Review, Quarterly West, The Rumpus, The Lifted Brow, DIAGRAM*, and an apocalyptic anthology called *Last Night on Earth*. He edited *Keyhole Magazine* and *Dark Sky Magazine*. Gabe lives in Los Angeles, CA, and *FUN CAMP* is his first book.

RECENTLY FROM PGP

I Don't Know I Said by Matthew Savoca, a novel

A Mountain City of Toad Splendor, a book of poetry and short fictions by Megan McShea

Night Moves, a conceptual ode by Stephanie Barber

Proving Nothing to Anyone by Matt Cook, a book of poems in five sections

Meat Heart, poetry by Melissa Broder

Old Gus Eats, a chapbook by Polly Duff Bresnick

Pee On Water, short stories by Rachel B. Glaser

Fog Gorgeous Stag, a book of whatsits by Sean Lovelace

please visit www.publishinggenius.com